TEKLA'S EASTER

STORY BY LILLIAN BUDD

PICTURES BY ·GENIA·

RAND McNALLY & COMPANY

CHICAGO   NEW YORK   SAN FRANCISCO

To DEBORAH and GUY

Far away, on the shore of a little island off the western coast of Sweden, the sea was singing. The song it sang was Mother Nature's Lullaby:

Oo—Oo—oo—swish—

Oo—Oo—oo—oo—splash!

Oo—Oo—oo—swish—

Over and over again, it sang:

Oo—Oo—oo—swish—

When a huge wave came it sang a wild, high note as it broke over the rocks of the little island's shore.

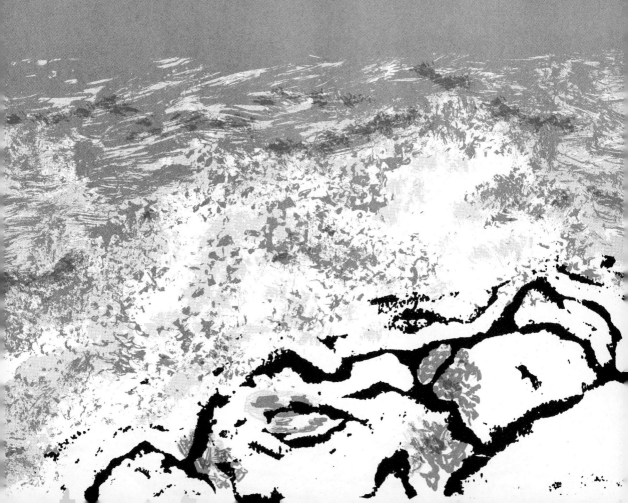

On the shore the water rolled, and broke, and burst into a bubbly foam.

High above the shore line there was a little red house, with white trim. Smoke rose quietly from its stone chimney.

Inside the small red house Tekla sat at a table. She was eight years old, going on nine.

Tekla was making a witch out of straw.

She had finished three. They stood on the table in front of her. If straw witches can watch their maker work, that was what they were doing.

Elsa, Tekla's five-year-old sister, already was asleep.
So was her big brother, Erik. He was nine, going on ten.

But Tekla had work to finish before she could go to bed. She had promised to make four straw witches to bring to the auction tomorrow afternoon.

Where Tekla lived, there was always an auction on Easter Eve to raise money for the school lunchroom.

Tekla's fingers tied knots in the string around the witch's waist, tied them tight, and cut off the ends.

She shivered. She had heard the story of the witches many times from the grown-ups. Long ago, when people believed in witches, they said that on the night before Good Friday all of the witches in the land began to gather at Blåkulla Mountain for a feast with the devil.

Where was Blåkulla?

Tekla smiled, remembering. She had looked and looked. She had even borrowed Grandfather's reading glass to help her search all over the map of Sweden, but she had not been able to find Blåkulla. Then she had asked Father. He told her it was the imaginary place in which the devil was king.

It was to Blåkulla that the witches flew through the air on long brooms. Each broom had a big black coffee pot hanging on it.

Some of the witches had black cats riding on their broomsticks, too.

Tonight the witches would have their feast at Blåkulla, the home of the devil, at the hour of midnight.

Grandmother had seen to it that the fire in the fireplace was out before sunset. She had closed the damper tight, so no witch could come down *her* chimney.

It seemed that Grandmother still half believed . . .

Again Tekla shivered. *So did she!*

Now Tekla cut a coffee pot from black paper and hung it on the little straw broom. She tied a cloth kerchief around the straw head.

The fourth witch was finished.

Tekla stood it beside the others.

Then she kissed her parents good-night and crept into her bunk bed.

"Wake up, Tekla! It's Easter Eve!" said Erik, as he bent over the bunk bed.

Easter Eve!

Up Tekla jumped.

"Wake up, Elsa!" Tekla called. "It is Easter Eve—the day of the auction!"

"The day we shoot off firecrackers to scare the witches of darkness away!" Erik added.

Erik ran to the door, opened it, and threw a firecracker on the ground, making an awful noise.

Elsa stuffed her fingertips into her ears. She did not like the noise of firecrackers. She liked dolls.

Then Elsa saw Tekla's doll. Tekla had forgotten to put it away.

Elsa picked it up.

"She's *mine*!" Tekla said, crossly, and tore the doll from her sister's arms.

She went to the storage room and put the doll inside a large chest with a heavy lid.

Elsa was very unhappy.

Tekla fixed a box lunch for her to take to the auction. But even this did not make Elsa gay.

Tekla noticed, but it *was* her doll! Anyway, she was too busy to care. She must get something from Mother and Grandmother to bring with her witches to the auction. Any little thing would do that would help raise money for the lunchroom fund.

At last they were all ready to go.

The sad look did not leave Elsa's eyes, even when the auction started. Quietly she stayed close to Tekla's side.

It seemed that everyone was here.

The boys' firecrackers went "Bang! Bang!"

The people bid "10 *öre* (or pennies), 20 *öre*, 30 *öre* . . ."

The auctioneer chanted: "Who'll bid 40—am I bid 50?" Then he called, "Going, going, GONE!"

Tekla was happy. She saw that each of her four witches had brought top price, 50 *öre*.

When the auction was over, the children left, though they all wished they could stay.

Tekla held Elsa by the hand. But they didn't go home right away. They stayed at the edge of the crowd.

Tekla was thinking: "Why can't I stay? Why am I not big enough to stay to dance around the Easter fires?"

The older boys had collected tar barrels. They had
carried them to the highest place on the highest hill. Tonight
they would stack one on top of the other, like a smokestack.
Then they would set fire to them.
The smoke would be very thick and very black. It would
be enough to scare any witch away, even without the flames.

If a barrel rolled off and tumbled down the rocky slopes, no one would care.

That would be even more fun. It would be very exciting.

There was no danger. They were always careful to see that nothing burnable would be in the way. But it was great fun when they all ran away, screaming.

Many fathers would be there to see that nothing bad happened.

The young people would dance all night around the fires. Then they would sit on the slopes, waiting breathlessly for the sun to rise on Easter Sunday morning.

Tekla and Elsa walked slowly away from the older boys and girls.

Late that evening, at home, Tekla forgot to wish she was older. Even Elsa forgot about the doll and was happy.

The girls were busy dressing up in witches' clothing— black and scary. So were other girls in houses all over Sweden.

Erik, and other Swedish boys, dressed all in black, too. They even blackened their faces with soot.

High-tailed black cats, made of yarn, clung to the tips of their broomsticks. Coffee pots (empty, to be sure) hung on the broom handles.

The three children screamed witches' screams as they climbed on their broomsticks.

They rode their broomsticks out into the night.

The girls half believed they *were* witches, chased away by the Easter fires and popping firecrackers. Even if they didn't really believe, they pretended they were rushing away from Blåkulla. They would stay hidden and quiet until next year.

For, when the sun rose, it would be Easter Sunday. With Easter day, the light and new life of Spring would come once more to the Swedish countryside.

"Wake up!" Again Erik bent over Tekla's bunk bed.

She jumped up quickly and awakened Elsa.

"Easter is a happy, happy day!" Erik was saying. "Don't you remember? Today is the one day in the whole year when we may eat all the eggs we can."

Was Erik always hungry, Tekla wondered.

Of course she remembered all about last Easter Sunday, when she was only seven. She remembered the Easter eggs, and the story-telling.

But she remembered best about the church boat.

She had sat in the middle seat, between Mother and Grandfather. And the long boat had gone gliding over the water . . .

Erik was dressed.

While Mother helped Elsa dress, Tekla drew on long red stockings. She put on fancy shoes with wooden soles, and heels almost under the middle of the foot. These were old-time shoes, handed down from a little girl of long ago.

On Easter day all of the people who lived on the island dressed up in the old-time costumes. On Easter day it was no regular Sunday church-going. It was like a festival.

Tekla slipped white linen petticoats over her head. She put on the blue skirt, the white linen blouse, the fancy, tight bodice, and the white apron and cap.

Now Tekla was ready to go to church. Soon the rest of the family were ready, too.

Leading the way for the others, Tekla and Erik walked to the boat landing. It was built on the landward side of the island, facing the mainland. The water was more gentle here than on the seaward side.

Swish—swish, the water said.

No matter how many times Tekla walked here, there were always many new things to see. When she was only as old as Elsa, Erik had told her that this was "adventure."

Tekla liked "adventure."

Now she forgot all about witches and Easter fires and Blåkulla. *They were going to ride in the church boat,* and that was even more exciting.

This was something they did only on Easter Sunday. On that day the islanders went to the big church on the mainland. On other Sundays they attended the little stone church on their island.

"Happy Easter," their neighbors greeted them, and they answered, "Happy Easter!"

They all chose seats in the long, narrow church boat.

The men had made the graceful boat. It was a copy of the beautiful old church boats that once were used on lakes in central Sweden.

Erik helped Mother into the boat, then sat down beside her. Father sat on the seat in front of them, with Grandmother. Grandfather sat on the seat in front of those two with Elsa. That left the single seat, in the very front, for—

"For me?" Tekla asked, in surprise. "For *me*?"

"For you," said Father and Grandfather, both in one breath.

"This is a happy day," Tekla said to herself.

She was to sit *in the prow*!

Tekla turned her head to look at all the people in the boat. Her family and the neighbors wore colorful shirts and dresses and head coverings.

But not all was color. The young oarsman, standing in the stern of the long boat, was dressed all in black. His coat had long swallow-tails.

With his high, black, stove-pipe hat, he looked almost as tall as a grandfather pine tree.

Tekla watched him guide the boat with his one long oar.

She felt Grandfather's tight hold on her belt. So she leaned toward the side of the boat, low in the water.

She let her arm hang over the side.

The water was cool and inviting.

S-W-I-S-H, S-W-I-S-H. Her fingers dragged in the water and made ripples. The ripples sparkled in the sunlight.

They reached the mainland and walked into the church.
Oh, thought Tekla, it is a happy thing to go to church
and sing!

She listened hard as the minister said: "Easter is a season of new life."

Then came another hymn, and the Easter service was over.

Outside, Mother put her
arm around Tekla's shoulders.
"Easter is all around us,"
Mother said. "See, over there?
Even last Sunday that was a
shiny, icy place. Today it is
a water puddle. The ice of
Winter has gone with the
coming of Easter."

Birds came and dipped their bills, and lifted them to let the water run down into their throats. Then they dipped them again, and again.

Or, Tekla wondered, was it that the birds were bowing? Bowing in thankfulness for the warm sunshine?

Mother pointed. "Look, Tekla, do you see the leaf buds on the birch trees?"

Tekla saw that they were swelling, getting ready to burst open. And they were beginning to turn green.

"That is what the minister meant, when he told us Easter brings new life," Mother said.

All winter the trees had been black against the sky. All Winter the snow had covered the ground. Now the warmth of the sun was pulling grass spears through.

Father spoke. "The sun's warmth is bringing new life to everything," he said. "Now that Easter has come, the whole world is re-borning."

"But Easter means more than new life," Erik said to her. "It means eating eggs for breakfast—all you can hold! M-m-m-"

Tekla knew. And she knew, too, that when you were a few years older, Eastertime meant going to watch the Easter fires on the mountain—the blazing fires that chased away the witches of darkness!

Then, when boys and girls grew to be young men and women, Eastertime meant dancing around the witch fires. And, sitting, waiting for the dawn.

"Hurry, Tekla." Erik took her hand. "Let's run to the boat."

As they ran, she asked him, "Don't you want to be the one to sit in the prow, going back home? I'll—I'll—let you, Erik."

He didn't even hear her. He was saying, half aloud, half under his breath, "I'm going to eat all the eggs I want!"

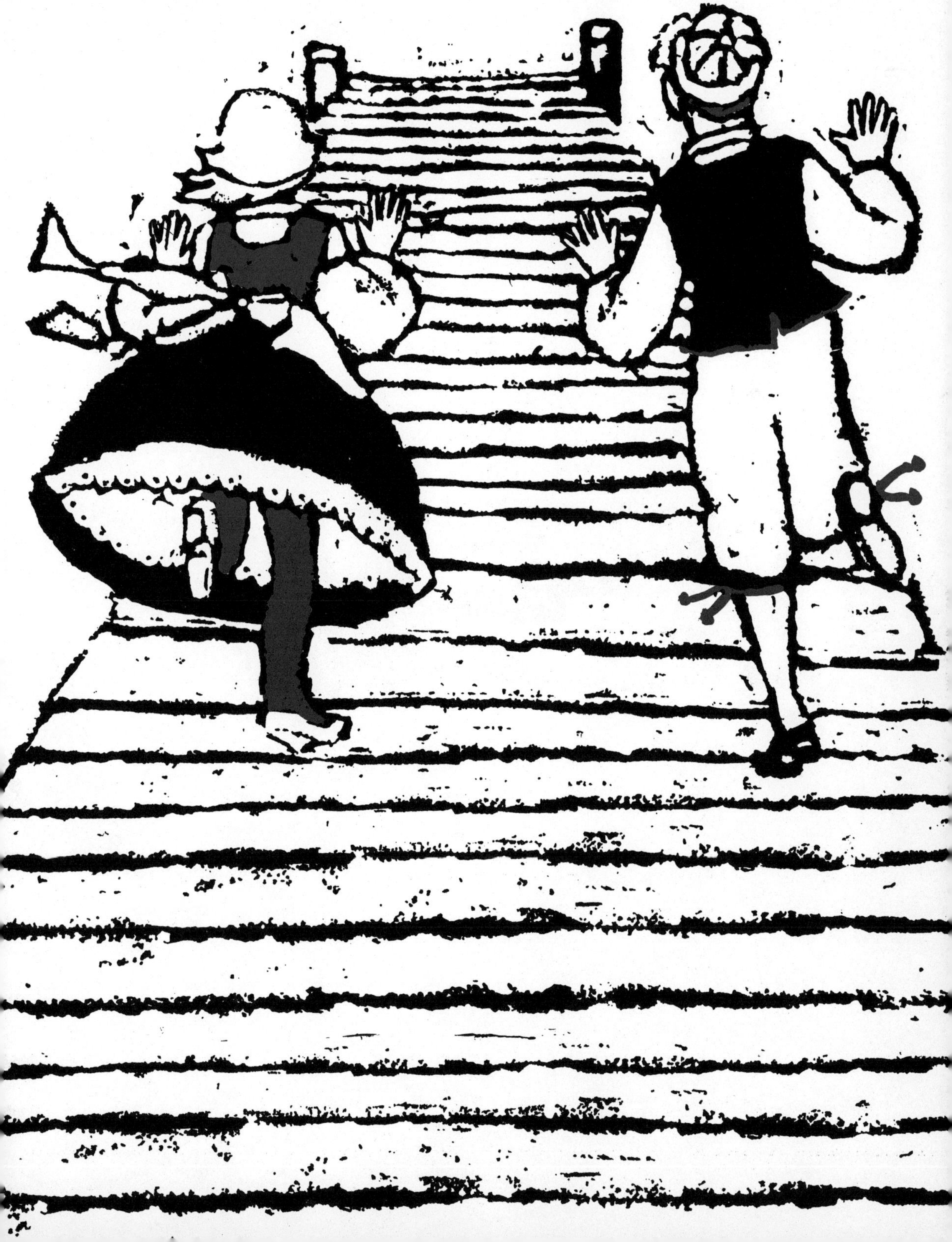

On the way home the oarsman guided the boat so smoothly Tekla felt as if everything else was moving, but that they were standing still.

Was this adventure? It was more like magic. The island, the shore line, the trees, the boat landing, her little red house —all were coming to meet *her*, instead of her moving toward them!

The children ran from the boat landing to the house. On the breakfast table were the Easter flowers. Mother showed Tekla how she had tied chicken feathers to the tips of birch twigs so they would look like garden flowers. But they were not ordinary chicken feathers, straight from the barn.

Oh, no! Mother had dyed these feathers yellow, and red, and blue. Even the pretty violet color was there.

Tiny green birch leaves sprouted up the stems. From a little distance away the fluffy feather flowers looked as if they might have grown in a garden.

As Tekla and her family chose their places at the table, other families, all over Sweden, would be sitting down to breakfast, too.

Erik could hardly wait to start eating.

But first, in this family as in many others, came the telling of Bible stories. This, too, was part of Easter for them. Mother carried in a small wooden bowl filled with eggs.

Such eggs! The insides had been blown out, so the eggs would last for years as keepsakes. On each one Mother had painted a picture telling a story from the Bible.

Each person at the table chose an egg. Then, if he told the story of the picture, he could keep the egg.

If anyone could not tell the story of his egg, he had to put the egg back into the bowl. He would not, then, have a souvenir of this year's Easter day.

"I'm going to eat all the hard-boiled eggs I can," Erik boasted.

But Grandfather was telling the first story: it was the story of Easter. He passed his egg around, for all to see. On it was the Cross. He told of the Resurrection, of re-borning, of Spring after Winter.

Father told the story of the Three Wise Men.

Erik told of Jonah and the whale.
Tekla had to laugh at that picture—a tiny little Jonah standing in an open mouth almost as big as the whole egg!

Elsa chose the one with Jesus holding a shepherd's staff in one hand, and a little lamb in the crook of His other arm. "The Lord is my Shepherd," she repeated proudly.

And now it was Tekla's turn.

She knew which one she was going to choose. She stopped her hand over one egg after another in the bowl, as if she were making up her mind. But she knew that she was going to choose the egg that showed a picture of the Infant Jesus.

She passed her egg around for everyone to see. Then she told her story.

After each one had earned his beautiful souvenir egg, Mother passed a large bowl of hard-boiled eggs. The bowl went around the table many times. Everyone ate and ate. But Erik ate more eggs than anyone else.

Tekla wondered how Grandfather had been able to eat any eggs, for he kept on telling Bible stories. Father tipped his chair back and sat listening. Tekla was so busy listening that she almost forgot to eat.

The stories Grandfather told made Tekla feel good. They made her feel like loving everybody in the whole wide world.

Then she saw that Elsa was crying. Because she was the smallest, she couldn't eat as many eggs as the others.

Tekla said to herself, "Poor Elsa. She is still a little girl."

Tekla excused herself from the table. She went to the storage room and opened the big chest. Tenderly she lifted her doll.

"Jonna, my darling," she whispered.

She sat cross-legged on the floor, rocking the doll, singing softly to it, and thinking. Elsa had always looked at Jonna with wishful eyes.

Tekla hugged the doll to her. Jonna was *her* doll! How often she had told Elsa that.

But, today, she had been big enough to sit in the prow of the church boat.

She brushed the matted hair back from Jonna's forehead. "Elsa will love you, too," she said, and carried the doll into the big room.

Smiling, Tekla held out the doll to her sister.

Night came.

The others lay in their beds, sleeping. Erik's broomstick, black cat and all, stood at the head of his bunk bed. The doll was cuddled in Elsa's arms.

But Tekla lay awake. There was so much thinking to do.

In her imagination, it was again Easter Eve.

The light from the embers in the fireplace became the light of the Easter fires. They burned, brightly, on the mountain top, scaring away the witches of darkness. The darkness of Winter soon would be gone.

The firelight made dancing patterns on the walls and ceiling of the big room. It was like seeing the sunshine on little ripples of water, as she had seen them while riding in the church boat.

Erik was right. Easter was a happy, happy day. And Father was right, except that it was not only a day for re-borning. It was a day for growing up. Today she had been allowed to sit, by herself, in the prow of the church boat!

She closed her eyes, to see again the world *coming toward her*.

Only a few more Easters and she would be big enough to dance with the young people around the Easter fires on the mountain top.

And then she would sit on the slopes, waiting for the sun to rise.

Imagining, Tekla heard the voices of happy young people come ringing in her ears.

And the voice of the murmuring sea whispered a lullaby.

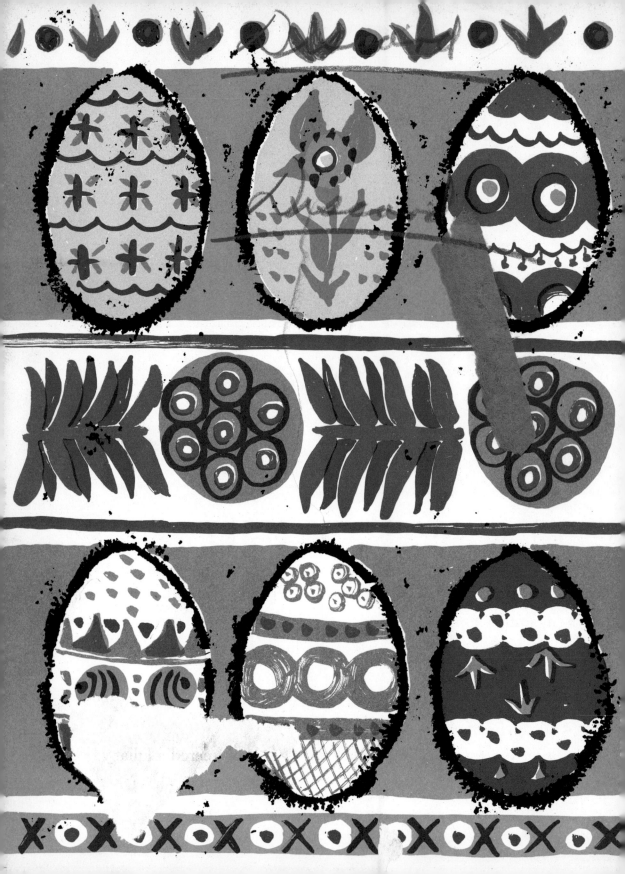